This book
belongs to:

_____

Read Along with Blue!

Based on the TV series *Blue's Clues*® created by Traci Paige Johnson,
Todd Kessler, and Angela C. Santomero as seen on Nick Jr.®
On *Blue's Clues*, Joe is played by Donovan Patton.
Photos by Joan Marcus.

SIMON SPOTLIGHT

An imprint of Simon & Schuster Children's Publishing Division
1230 Avenue of the Americas, New York, New York 10020
My Dress-up Party and *My Visit with Periwinkle*
copyright © 2003 Viacom International Inc.
Blue's Beach Day and *Hello, Spring!*
copyright © 2004 Viacom International Inc.
Hooray for Polka Dots! copyright © 2005 Viacom International Inc.

Manufactured in the United States of America
8 10 9 7
ISBN-13: 978-1-4169-0626-1
ISBN-10: 1-4169-0626-6

These titles were previously published individually
by Simon Spotlight.

Read Along with Blue!

Ready-to-Read

Simon Spotlight/Nick Jr.

New York   London   Toronto   Sydney

Contents

Hello, Spring!

by Alison Inches
illustrated by Ian Chernichaw

Good-bye, winter!

Good-bye, snow!

Good-bye, ice!

Good-bye, sled!

Good-bye, boots!

Good-bye, mittens!

Good-bye, hat!

Hello, spring!

Hello, sun!

Hello, ducks!

Hello, bugs!

Hello, worms!

Hello, swings!

Hello, slide!

Hello, baseball!

Hello, flowers!

Hello, birds!

Hello, bike!

Hello, kite!

I love spring!

Blue's Beach Day

by Jeff Borkin
illustrated by Karen Craig

We are at the beach today!

Ooh, the sand is hot!

But the water is cool.

Here is a good spot.

We will make a sand castle!

Shovel digs a hole.

Pail holds the sand.

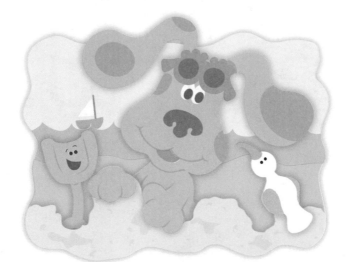

The sand castle
gets bigger . . .

and bigger!

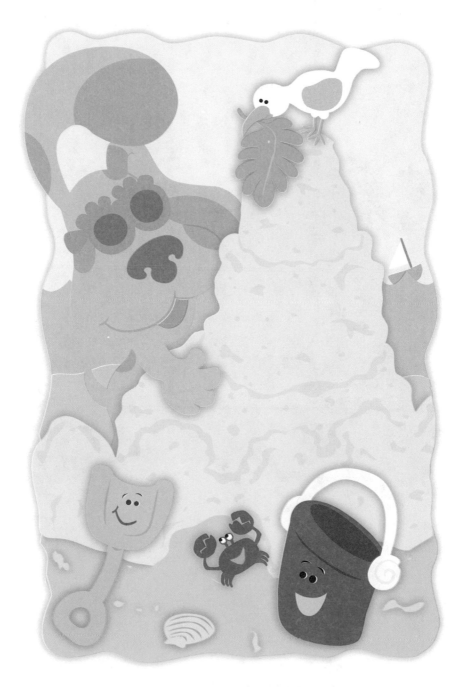

We find seashells
for the sand castle.

Ta da!
The sand castle
is done!

Now we wait.

The water comes
closer . . .

and closer.

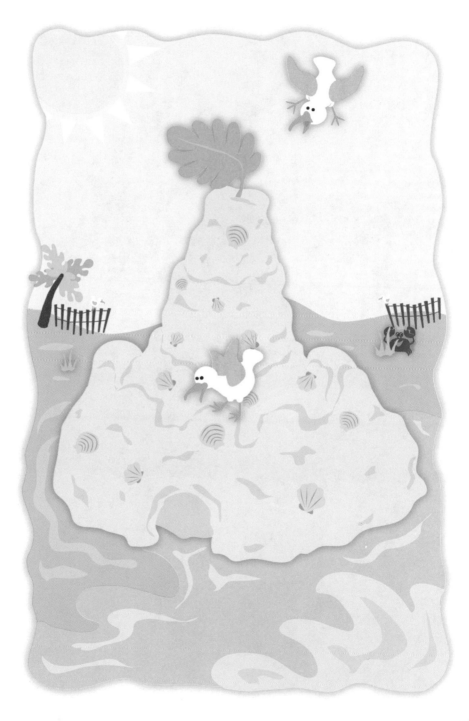

Sploosh!

Hooray!

My Dress-up Party

by Sarah Willson
illustrated by Jennifer Oxley

COSTUME BOX

Hi! I am 🐾 BLUE. We are having a dress-up party! Joe is hanging 🎈🎈 BALLOONS all over the 🏠 HOUSE.

Mr. Salt and Mrs. Pepper baked a .

CAKE

Paprika will scoop out the . Yum!

ICE CREAM

Now we can set the

TABLE with PLATES , FORKS ,

and SPOONS !

It is time to dress up!
Tickety Tock is going
as a grandfather 🕐.

CLOCK

Mailbox is wearing a costume.

Mr. Salt and Mrs. Pepper are dressed up as .

CHEFS

Paprika is going as a .

SPOON

65

Joe and I still need costumes. We can look in Joe's .

CLOSET

Maybe his  will give us an idea.

SHOES

He can be a ⚾ BASEBALL
player, an ice-skater,
or pretend he is
going to the 🏖 .
BEACH

Look at all the in my  .

HATS

COSTUME BOX

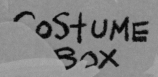

COSTUME BOX

I could be an  **ASTRONAUT** ,

a **FIREFIGHTER** , or a **FARMER** .

The guests are already at the !

Magenta came as a  .

PRINCESS

Periwinkle is wearing a 🎩 costume.

MAGICIAN

We still need costumes! What else is in my  ?

COSTUME BOX

I think Joe has an
idea. What could
he do with these

SOCKS ?

Now I am dressed like .

JOE

And Joe is dressed like me, !

BLUE

It is time for 🎩 *ICE CREAM* and 🍰 *CAKE*. Thank you for coming!

My Visit with Periwinkle

by Alison Inches
illustrated by David B. Levy

Hi! It is me, .
BLUE

Today [PERIWINKLE] is

coming to my [HOUSE]

for a visit.

81

When  gets
PERIWINKLE

here, we will have

, , and .
SANDWICHES   MILK   COOKIES

Then we are going to play in the  .

PARK

I made a 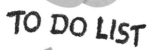 of

things to do before

comes over.

PERIWINKLE

1. Clean the  .
HOUSE

2. Make .
SANDWICHES

3. Put out MILK and .
MILK   COOKIES

TO DO LIST

1.

2.

3.

First we have to clean the

HOUSE

I need to put away my BLOCKS . I have █ RED blocks and █ BLUE blocks.

While Joe makes the ![BED], I hang up my ![PAJAMAS].

BED

PAJAMAS

They have  on them!

STARS

The  is clean.

HOUSE

Now it is time to make the .

SANDWICHES

TO DO LIST

1. ✔

2. —

3. —

 and  help me.

MR. SALT   MRS. PEPPER

 likes

PERIWINKLE   PEANUT BUTTER   SANDWICHES

I like  .

CHEESE SANDWICHES

Almost done! What is the last thing on my  ?

LIST

Put out  MILK and COOKIES !

The have
COOKIES   HEARTS

on them.

They make us smile.

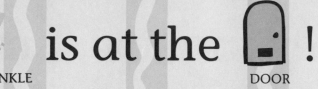

PERIWINKLE is at the DOOR !

He brought 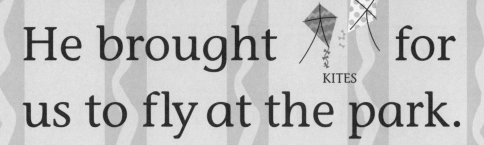 for us to fly at the park.

We can fly our KITES
right after lunch.

The  make
smile too!

COOKIES

PERIWINKLE

Look at our KITES flying in the sky! I love when PERIWINKLE visits.

Hooray for Polka Dots!

by Alison Inches
illustrated by Ian Chernichaw

Hi! It is me, . BLUE
Today I am going to the fair with my CLASS !

is coming

with us.

I love to go places

with  !

We are riding on the !
SCHOOL BUS
The SCHOOL BUS stops
at the fair GATE.

Wow! Look at all the rides!

MAGENTA wants to go on the **AIRPLANE** ride. **PERIWINKLE** wants to go on the **MERRY-GO-ROUND**.

I want to go
on the giant 🛝.

SLIDE

But first we eat
lunch.
We have 🍕 and 🧃.

PIZZA   JUICE

Yum!

Now it is time for rides! Yay!

"Wow! The go really high," says

.

MAGENTA

AIRPLANES

"Hold on to 🐨 !"
POLKA DOTS

I say.

"Then the ✈ will
AIRPLANES

not seem so high."

"Now I love the 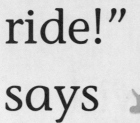 AIRPLANE

ride!"

says .

MAGENTA

"We love the AIRPLANE ride too!" say PERIWINKLE and I.

"The goes

MERRY-GO-ROUND

really fast,"

says .

PERIWINKLE

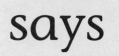

118

"Hold on to !"
POLKA DOTS
I say.
"Then the will
MERRY-GO-ROUND
not seem so fast."

"Now I love the 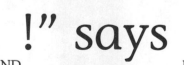!" says .

MERRY-GO-ROUND

PERIWINKLE

"We love the

MERRY-GO-ROUND

too!" say  and I.

MAGENTA

"Now it is my turn!"
I say.
I want to ride the
giant 🛝.

SLIDE

Wow! That 🛝 sure is tall!

SLIDE

"Hold on to  !"
say  and  .

POLKA DOTS

MAGENTA

PERIWINKLE

"Then the 🛝 will not seem so tall." Wheeeee!

"Now I LOVE the giant !" I say.
SLIDE
"We do too!" say  and .
PERIWINKLE   MAGENTA
Hooray for !
POLKA DOTS